SANTA'S UNIVERSAL FAMILY TALES

A FAMILY REUNION

KEITH A. STAFFORD

*I dedicate this book to my wife-Miriam,
14 children, 20 grandchildren, and 6
great-grandchildren, at this time.*

*I thank The Most High for Blessing my health to
continue this life journey and thanks to all my doctors
at St. Jude/Providence Medical Center, Fullerton, CA.*

*Special thanks to my Book Team: Marti Melville, Patrica
Brack, Holly Carton, Fiona Jayde, Tamara Cribley, and to
my Music Team: Michael Mani, Jay R, Kathleen Thomas,
Craig White, Peter Humphreys, Sundail Agency, Neal
Sapper, Allen Kepler, Doug Sinclair, Patty Jackson, Donny
D and Rick Scott: GREAT SCOTT P.R.ODUCTIONS.*

*Thank you to my Inspiration Team: my awesome Church
Family Worldwide, Realty One Group West-Anaheim,
CA, Belton Mouras Entertainment (Belton & Lola
Mouras, Jr.) Sacramento, CA, 100 Block North 61st
St. Neighborhood Philadelphia, PA, Tony Saunders &
Family, Lorraine Evanoff, Chef Curtis Akins, Sr., and
finally All My Friends & Family across the globe!*

Meet the Claus Family

SANTA CLAUS – 21st Century as we all know and love him today.

MRS. CLAUS – Behind every good Santa there's an awesome Mrs. Claus.

NANA CLAUS – the matriarch of the Claus family. She always keeps the Legacy alive!

MATILDA – Oldest adopted elf daughter.

SAINT NICHOLAS – Oldest cousin and brother-like, who keeps the records of children's good and nice deeds.

 BLACK PETER – Chimney sweep by day and a close cousin to the Claus family. He keeps the records of children's "naughty deeds" and delivers the proper letter to encourage and inspire good will and obedience.

 SAINT LUCIA – The brave and heroic woman, who saved the children from hunger serving warm cakes, lussekatter, ginger biscuits, and hot drinks for children during the cold winter months.

 KENTE CLAUS – Known as the Ambassador of Goodwill, spreading love, peace and unity in all communities globally. Did you know, Kente Claus has walked in the Macy's Thanksgiving Day Parade on behalf of the Claus Family? You might just see him there one day!

 PAPA NOEL – He brings a joyful spirit and heartfelt tunes to Santa's Universal Family Tales, teaching children the importance of music, togetherness, and the traditions of storytelling and gratitude.

Thanksgiving Eve had finally arrived

With more to the hubbub that felt almost alive.

With hope and eagerness that buzzed through the house.

For now the world waited, as still as a mouse.

What lie ahead, during holiday times?

Can only be found in memos and jingle-bell chimes.

And do you, dear reader, look into the skies?

There's wonder and love there when you open your eyes...

Nana Claus, Matilda, Santa, Mrs. Claus

Chapter One

Thanksgiving Eve had finally arrived. A sparkle of twinkling lights laced along the outside windows, only added to the magic of the night. The Claus family was different.

"I see you in there," Mrs. Claus said and winked. A little hand snatched a loose bit of confection, not yet ready for the table, and popped it into her mouth. "Santa will certainly put you on the Naughty List!"

"No, he won't!" the little voice shouted out, giggling as she darted into the next room to hide with the other elves.

Indeed, the Claus home was aglow with the spirit of the season and the warmth of family togetherness. Magic seemed to happen every year during the holiday season, woven in unison with joy and love for one another.

"As it should be," Mrs. Claus said aloud. She glanced at the twinkling lights draped across the fireplace mantle and smiled. Beams sparkled from every corner of the great room.

"Preparations are coming together, Mamma," Santa Claus' voice was deep and full and seemed to always follow a bear-hug.

"Thank you, Papa. Many hands make light work. We're lucky to have such a big, wonderful family!"

Mrs. Claus sniffed, wiping her eyes, then wandered over to the oversized oven and peered in.

"Santa's at the sticky buns again!" Matilda swatted his hand with her apron just as he opened the oven door.

"They're not ready yet, dear," Mrs. Claus announced and stomped her foot. That was her cue for others to leave the kitchen. Indeed, there were many hands at work and Santa's weren't welcome…not yet.

He chuckled and a hearty "Ho-Ho-Ho!" echoed throughout the kitchen. "Matilda, you are a force to be reckoned with." He gave Matilda a squeeze, snatched a sugared plum, and chuckled again.

"Go make yourself useful, Papa. The fireplace needs to be stoked and the reindeer need carrots, methinks," Mrs. Claus announced.

Santa made his way to the fireplace and snatching up a log, placed it into the flames. The room instantly smelled of pine and cinnamon, a custom Matilda learned centuries ago to scent the yule logs.

The house continued to buzz with excitement to match the crackling of the fire. Santa smiled and relished thoughts of the season –Thanksgiving would be the first celebration, followed by the countdown to that very special day called Christmas. This celebration would be the best they ever had…he just knew it.

"Truly, the most *joyous* and *thankful* time of the year!" he whispered.

Nana Claus, Mrs. Claus, Santa

Chapter Two

"**P**ass the pickled turnips, please!"

No one responded to the request. A second time, the turnips were besought and a second time, no one responded. Perhaps it was because of the clanking of dishes and garrulous chatter that carried across the long, oak table where the Claus family ate Thanksgiving dinner.

A-hemmm, Santa cleared his throat and the chatter died down. "Boris has something to say." Santa nodded to the elf who stood upright, nose touching the edge of the table. "You'd better stand on your chair so that we all can see you better, Boris," Santa added.

Boris climbed up and stood nearly three feet tall atop his chair. His growly and very deep voice caught everyone's attention. "I would like the pickled turnips, please."

All eyes darted to Nana Claus. Santa glanced at his mother.

Nothing happened. Nana Claus just sat there, eyes focused on some far-away place, unblinking, and misty.

"Mamma…our dear Boris has kindly requested you pass the turnips. They're right there in front of you," Santa said.

Still nothing.

"*Maaa-maaaa!*" Boris sang out, "Please pass the turnips!"

At the sound of his voice, she jumped. "Oh! My dear, sweet boy! Here, let me get that for you." She took hold of the silver dish and passed it to Mavis, a gentle elf and an expert at painting the eyelashes on baby dolls. Mavis passed the dish to Albert, the reindeer's antler and hoof polisher, who passed it to the next elf, and then the next until it reached Boris.

"Thank you!" Boris said and took his seat. He helped himself to a heaping pile of pickled turnips and potatoes, and then said, "You know how I love pickled turnips and potatoes with gravy."

Santa leaned over to Nana Claus. "Are you feeling alright, ma? You seemed to be elsewhere a moment ago."

"She's fine, dear," Mrs. Claus said and touched her husband's arm. "Nana Claus is lost in thought."

Nana Claus sniffed back a tear. "Oh, Santa…I was. I was deep in a daydream." She gazed at the bustling elves—her adopted grandchildren—and glanced out the window where the majestic reindeer rested just outside.

"What is wrong? This is a festive time for *love, peace, unity* and thanks-giving. That's what this magnificent feast is called, you know…*Thanks-Giving*." Santa gave her hand a squeeze.

"Oh, I know…I know. And I am very thankful. We have such a beautiful family and I love you and all my children, including the furry ones too! But I feel that we're missing someone…actually, missing a few."

"Elves? More elves?" Santa looked confused. "Mamma. Our table won't hold many more. We'd have to build another room and another table, not to mention all the chairs!"

Mrs. Claus smiled and patted Santa's hand. "It's difficult to explain. She has memories."

"Yes! Mrs. Claus is correct. It's a feeling in my heart—a deep yearning to bring together our family. Santa, the legacy has remained fragmented for far too long."

Santa's eyes grew wide. "You mean, the Brotherhood of Santas."

Nana Claus nodded and a tear rolled slowly, glistening on her cheek.

Nana Claus, Mrs. Claus, Santa

Chapter Three

"Cousins," Mrs. Claus whispered.

"What did you say?" Santa looked confused. "Cousins?"

Mrs. Claus nodded. "Yes, dear husband…and sidekicks."

Santa looked more confused than ever. He scratched his head and the curls in his white hair bounced around his shoulders. "I'm going to go see what Matilda's doing with the sticky buns. I'll leave you and Nana to her thoughts." He stood and scooted into the kitchen.

But Nana Claus hardly noticed. Her eyes stared at the twinkling lights along the mantle. Unblinking, her gaze grew soft and she drifted off to another time, another place. As her thoughts wandered, cherished recollections of Santa's childhood friends and family carried her into precious memories. Remembrances of sidekicks and secret cousins, who shared mischievous adventures in days long gone.

Oh, they were the naughty ones…those mischievous cousins of his! The thought made her chuckle but didn't break the spell. With each passing moment, she envisioned the many faces of Santa's childhood family members, each with their own unique gifts and mythical stories.

One by one, she whispered their names: "Deacon Saint Nicholas—a generous saint who loved the children," she paused and smiled, "Black Peter, the playful cousin that would keep the list of misbehaving children…"

"But always encouraged them to *Do Right*, or else there would be consequences." Mrs. Claus added.

Nana paused again and chuckled. Her daughter-in-law was correct. Something about Black Peter's unique streetwise, reasoning style that seemed a perfect balance to the Deacon Saint. "He works well with the Sinterklaas, methinks. Too bad the Bavarians turned the Krampus into such a scary character."

In that moment, Santa peeked in on her from around the oversized archway that led to the kitchen. "Everything alright in there?"

Nana nodded. "Just reminiscing, Santa…just reminiscing." He touched his nose and nodded (a rather common habit for Santa just before he disappears up a chimney) and vanished back into the kitchen.

Nana Claus slipped back to her memories and her list of names. "Saint Lucia. She was such a brave heroine. Those hungry children were truly saved by her warm, yummy cakes and delightful oat milk during the harsh winter months so many years ago. Indeed, Saint Lucia's memory still shines light on dark, cold days…yes it does!"

Mrs. Claus nodded in agreement. They sat for a moment in silence, envisioning each of the cousins' faces, and another tear rolled down Nana's cheek.

"Why are you so sad, Nana?" Mrs. Claus asked.

Nana's look seemed far away as she spoke. "Because it's been too long. There is so much time lost and our family needs to be reunited. Do you think it could ever happen?"

Just then, Mrs. Claus clapped her hands and stood with a new determination. She marched to the same archway where Santa had been peering at her only moments ago.

Then, in her loudest voice, she called out. "Santa! We have work to do. Call in your reindeer. It's time to make this happen!"

Santa, Reindeer

Chapter Four

"Your harness is a bit tight, Vixen. Have you been nippin' at the oats again?" Gunnar grinned. As the sturdiest elf, he always tended to the livestock—mainly the reindeer, which were his favorites.

Vixen snorted and flicked his tail.

"Don't get grumpy with me. I didn't feed 'em to you." Gunnar scratched Vixen between the ears, causing the reindeer to chuff. There was a rustle of hooves in the next stall. "You're next, Dasher."

"I've got him," Boris' deep voice rolled from the barn door. "I'm going along anyway." He moved into Dasher's stall and began to fasten the antique harness around Dasher's neck. Bells jingled and the other reindeer shook their heads and pawed the ground in anticipation. Harness bells always meant a significant trip somewhere.

"Where are we going? Do you know?"

"Nana said something about cousins and an important message. I guess we're going to see some of Santa's relatives," Boris replied.

As the two elves finished preparing the reindeer, Nana Claus made her way into the barn. She nodded her approval and stroked Prancer's mane. "Looking just perfect, crew."

Just then, Santa walked in carrying a satchel and a strange-looking package. It wasn't wrapped in the typical holiday paper but rather, a burlap sack that was tied with twine. Tucked into a knot was a tiny, red-striped candy cane.

"Did the messages get sent, Einar?" Santa glanced at the plucky, little elf with the mailman's hat. "It's extremely important that…"

"Almost, Santa," Einar interrupted. "The various messages are being prepared now. We should have them en route to their recipients in…" Einar paused to look at his rather elaborate watch, "…in about 30 seconds."

"Most excellent! I can always rely on you to deliver the mail in whatever form it goes, Einar." Santa winked.

The chime of the Claus Clock sounded behind them, exactly eight times. On cue, jingle bells rang and tiny wooden dancers in curly shoes and tall hats began to tap and twirl around the giant clock's base. It was time.

"Messages sent!" Einar announced as the last jingle bell rang out.

Santa glanced at the sky and saw a faint sprinkle of snow and ash pass through a puffy cloud—the residue left from the high-speed of the traveling messages. "Well done," Santa said and turned back to preparing the sleigh.

"I've got a few people to see on the way. Those messages will set the stage and prepare my cousins for an unexpected guest."

Santa grinned. "A bit of old-time, holiday fun-time!"

Black Peter

Chapter Five

The sun dipped below the erratic silhouette of scant trees that hugged the winding roads that led to the village. Peter had just returned from his latest chimney sweep. Soot floated in tiny wisps behind him, caught in the remaining light of the waning dusk. Soon it would be dark and Peter would barely be seen, should he venture out—due in part to the ash and soot that covered his face and arms. As a chimney sweep, it was part of the job to get covered in ash, darkening every part of Peter's skin, and earning him the nickname, "Black Peter."

As he approached his favorite chair, he noticed something odd lying against the bricks lining the fireplace. He looked at the package and shook his head.

"Well," he said to himself. "What have we here?" He stopped and stared at the burlap tied with twine. Tucked in the knot was a tiny candy cane. "Most interestingly… how did you get here?"

Black Peter chuckled and glanced around the room. "I know you're here Kris. Come out of hiding like the good Santa you are."

From the corner, behind a drape, black boots protruded beneath. "Ho! Ho! Ho!" rang out as Santa stepped free of the drapery and greeted Peter. "How'd you find me."

"Well, you've never been very good at hide-n-seek!" Peter replied. "Hello cousin!"

"Greetings Pete! It's been a very long time since we've shared a roaring fire together, hasn't it?" Santa grinned and moved to the fireplace, warming his hands as he spoke.

"Indeed, it has. Far too long," the response came from the doorway where Nana Claus stood. "It's about time you two get together, you know."

"Nana!" Black Peter rushed over to hug her but she stopped him short.

"Not until you clean yourself up, Peter. I don't want to travel in that sleigh with soot attached to me."

Peter chuckled. "I don't blame you." His eyes darted between his guests. "To what do I have the pleasure of your company this evening?"

Nana Claus nodded to Santa who picked up the package and handed it to Peter. "This is for you."

Peter held the package and stared at Santa. "But why? It's not Christmas…nor my birthday."

"For heaven's sake, open it, Peter!" Nana Claus' voice had that tone that suggested she not be trifled with. "It's the start of the holiday season and we've been thinking about your childhood years."

Peter pulled the twine and placed the candy cane in his mouth. *Mmmm.* The burlap fell away revealing a broom. "I don't understand," Peter said. "You know I have several of these. Why…?"

"That is not just any chimney sweep broom, Pete. It's got a bit of holiday magic attached to it," Santa replied.

Peter stared at the broom that glinted gold sparkles of light as he turned it in his hand. It was indeed an unusual broom. "What do I do with it?"

"Sweep, of course," Santa said and winked, motioning to Peter's chimney. "And as you do, pay close attention to the walls inside that chimney of yours."

Santa, Black Peter

Chapter Six

Black Peter paused only a moment before he scrambled up his chimney. Fortunately, he wasn't bothered by the heat of a recent fire and enjoyed feeling his muscles and bones warmed inside the brick walls.

His chimney was rather clean, compared to most he swept, but then again, it would be, given that the chimney belonged to Black Peter's house. He allowed his eyes to adjust to the darkness, anticipating the pale light to filter in from the room where Santa rested, waiting patiently for Peter to sweep with the unusual broom.

As he glanced at the brick, he noticed a patch of ash stuck to one side of brick. As he lifted the broom, the ash began to move. It was as if the ash was trying to tell him something. Peter moved the bristles closer and the ash wriggled more rapidly.

"What is going on?" Peter said to himself. A resounding "Ho-Ho-Ho" echoed from below. Apparently, Santa knew a little more about this than he was willing to let on.

"Santa, what aren't you telling me?" Black Peter shouted.

"Just sweep, Pete!" came the response, followed by another "Ho!"

As instructed, Peter kept sweeping and as he did so, letters began to form in the ash. As they wriggled and moved together, words then full sentences appeared.

"A message? You sent me a message?" Peter shouted below to Santa. "Why couldn't you just tell me?"

Santa chuckled. "Because this is more fun!"

Peter continued to sweep and soon, the message became clear enough to read.

"What does it say?" Santa said.

"You know full well what it says," Peter hollered. "It…it…"

"Read it aloud," Santa insisted.

Peter squinted his eyes and began to read the words. "It's an invitation of some sort." He leaned in and recited the invitation loud enough for Santa to hear:

You are hereby, and very cordially invited, to a week-long visit in the North Pole, courtesy of Santa's Universal Family. Please bring appropriate attire and an appetite. We will be reuniting with other family members, so plan to share memories and old-time traditions as kin.

"A family reunion? You're inviting me to a family reunion?" Black Peter said as he slid down the flu. Standing with feet wide apart and hands on hips, Peter stared at Santa for a moment. Ash fell in gray sparkles from his jacket. "Seriously? A family reunion?"

Santa nodded and chuckled again.

Suddenly, Black Peter charged Santa, threw his arms around him, and sobbed. "I'm so happy! I can't wait."

In the doorway, Nana Claus looked at Santa and winked.

Saint Lucia

Chapter Seven

It was particularly cold outside and with frost slowly spreading along with traces of snow that had begun to fall. In truth, this ride would be quite challenging, but Santa loved challenges and his reindeer were always excited for new adventures. They pawed at the ground, anxious to get moving, aware that this expedition would be something unusual—a very unique and special journey.

"Let's get going, travel team. We've got a race against the weather," Santa announced. The elves scurried about, readying the reindeer for the flight. Everyone knew the importance of the message that needed to be delivered.

With frost gently painting Saint Lucia's windowpanes, traces of snow followed short bursts of wind that rustled the pine trees. She watched as a fluffy white Arctic fox darted into the thick brush that was its home.

"Stay with your babies tonight, mamma. It's chilly outside," she said, knowing the little fox would be snug and warm in its den. "Now, to make my own little home cozy."

Saint Lucia had already begun preparations for the annual celebration on December 13th. She couldn't help but feel excited as she walked to the fireplace and lit the kindling. Instantly, the scent of pine and cinnamon filled her cottage. Saint Lucia looked around her, searching for the one person she knew would scent her kindling with cinnamon. "Nana Claus? Are you here?"

No one answered.

She walked into the kitchen searching for Nana Claus. "Nana? Where are you?" Her search took her toward the oven and she noticed something unusual. "What in the world?"

Saint Lucia glanced down at a sparkling ivory plate painted with holly and berries. Set snugly in the center were tiny round cakes and thick slices of bread. "*Lussekatter* and ginger biscuits!" she squealed. "Oh! It's still early for saffron bread and ginger biscuits…and I'm the one who usually prepares these!" Glancing to the side, she saw a silver pot, steaming with the smell of melted chocolate. "And hot cocoa!"

Saint Lucia snatched a ginger biscuit from the plate and walked into the foyer then circled back into the room where the fireplace glowed with the fire she'd lit only moments ago.

"Someone…and I think I know who it is…brought me a holiday treat. The very treat that I bring to others. I wonder why?" She bit into the biscuit and relished the taste of ginger mixed with the scent of cinnamon wafting from her fireplace. Taking another bite, she sat in her favorite rocking chair and decided to simply enjoy the moment.

But as she chewed, something tasted rather unusual. "What in the world?" she said again and reached for a strange item sticking out of the middle of the biscuit. "What is this?"

She pulled on the end of a strip of paper that had been baked into the biscuit. Out slid a paper ribbon, exposing some elaborate scribbling written along its length. She held it up and began to read. "It's a message! Someone's sent me a secret message baked into a ginger biscuit… and they used my recipe to do it! Only one person has my recipe and it's likely the same person who scented my kindling! Nana Claus!"

Behind her, she heard shuffling followed by a low-pitched giggle. Someone was in her house and seemed to be watching her.

Nana Claus, Saint Lucia

Chapter Eight

"I spy with my big blue eyes…" Saint Lucia peeked around the edge of her oversized chair, "…a little elf with a great big grin!"

Katia jumped. She'd been hiding but simply couldn't hold back a burbly burst of giggles any longer. "I knew you'd find them! *Lussekatter* and ginger biscuits with cocoa are my favorites! You bring it to me every holiday season."

Lucia smiled and held her arms out to the little elf. "Yes…yes, I do. And this year you brought it to me."

Katia scrambled up to Lucia and gave her a hug. "I've missed you," she said.

"And I've missed you too!" Lucia replied. "I knew something was about to happen—something very good!

"Well, of course," Katia said. "You are the Lady of the Light in the family."

Saint Lucia smiled. "I think we all feel that special holiday feeling during this time, after the festivities of Thanksgiving. It means the holidays have finally arrived and more celebrations are about to happen!" She glanced around the room. "Now where is Nana Claus? I know she's around here somewhere." She glanced over her shoulder, hoping to catch a glimpse of the Clauses.

"Oh!" Katia squealed, distracted. She pointed to the half-eaten biscuit on a tea plate. "You found the message!"

Lucia nodded. "Yes, I did. I was about to read it. Would you like me to read it aloud for you to hear as well?" Katia nodded and sat in the puffy leather chair across from Lucia. Then, taking the slip of paper in her hands, she adjusted her reading spectacles on her nose and began:

You are hereby, and very cordially invited, to a week-long visit in the North Pole, courtesy of Santa's Universal Family. Please bring appropriate attire and an appetite. We will be reuniting with other family members, so plan to share memories and old-time traditions as kin.

P. S. We would also appreciate your famous, yummy, warm cakes to share.

When she had finished reading the note, Lucia dropped her hands into her lap. "Well, now…that is quite a message. I wonder who sent it?"

Katia giggled again, followed by the echo of a familiar "Ho-Ho-Ho!" from the kitchen. Katia clapped her hands for joy and in that instant, Nana Claus rushed in and wrapped her arms around Lucia. "I could barely keep myself still. I've been so excited to see you! Please say you'll come to our gathering."

Lucia glanced at her dear Nana Claus with tearful eyes. "I wouldn't miss it for the world!"

"And you *will* bring your warm cakes and cocoa, won't you…please?" Santa said. "We've missed those too…and you, sweet Saint Lucia!"

"Of course I will," she replied. "But I may need to borrow one of your elves to help me in the kitchen."

Katia's hand shot straight up in the air. "Oh, please Nana, please Santa! Let me stay with Auntie Lucia to help her. I know exactly how to make her ginger biscuits and I can melt the cocoa just right."

Santa winked at Nana Claus and nodded. "I think it would be fine for Katia to stay this time."

"But only if she helps you and promises to come back home, Lucia. She can travel with you when you come out for our gathering."

"Done!" Lucia and Katia said at the same time.

The fire crackled and all four family members shared ginger biscuits and cocoa. "Well, it doesn't hurt to start the holiday traditions a little early, now does it," Saint Lucia said and grinned then bit into a slice of buttered *Lussekatter*.

Saint Nicholas

Chapter Nine

Jingle bells hushed the wind as it raced through pine trees and danced over mistletoe just blooming with berries and blossoms. The ancient Lycian city of Patara was the only place anyone could hear the jingles. Most believe it's because that's where Saint Nicholas lived… and still does.

This day was especially magical as the bells sounded just a bit louder than their usual whisper. Something was in the air and it was more than just the jingle of bells. Saint Lucia had felt it and Saint Nicholas's elves had too.

"I'm not sure just what…but I agree, it feels different this morning," Nicholas said. "A mystical, holiday thrill, don't you think?"

The little elf standing at his side nodded.

"See there…the snowflakes have changed." Santa pointed to a flurry of flakes.

The little elf jumped up and down, clapping his hands. "Pink and green and blue!"

Indeed, the snowflakes had taken on the colors of a rainbow, pale and sparkly. They looked like tiny prisms falling from the sky. This only happened once a year—a sign that the magic of the holiday season had arrived.

Saint Nicholas tipped his head to listen to his reindeer in their stalls, restless and singing a throaty, grunting song that meant they, too, noticed the charmed morning.

"Look!" the little elf said, pointing to the trees. "What is that?" he said.

A group of colorful flakes had attached to the pines, much the same way ornaments are hung. But these flakes hung in a pattern, unlike anything Nicholas had ever seen before.

"Well, look at that!" Nicholas said and chuckled. "I've never noticed this materialize with snow. Let's take a look, shall we?" He marched through the snowy white that covered the ground to where glittery, colored snowflakes clung to the trees. Nicholas shook his head. "I can't tell what this means." He looked behind him but the little elf had suddenly disappeared.

"Here!" the tiny voice called from above.

Nicholas looked up to see the elf standing on the roof of the reindeer's barn. Antlered heads peered out of their stalls. The reindeer seemed to be grinning. "What are you doing up there, Andre?"

The little elf clapped hands and pointed. "You can see from up here. It's…it's…the snow has written something in the trees." Andre clapped again. "Come see. It's a message and it's for you!"

Santa, Saint Nicholas

Chapter Ten

"Well, will you look at that?" Saint Nicholas said. The reindeer snorted excitedly.

"I told you so!" Andre said, nearly dancing in place, and Nicholas chuckled.

"Yes, you did." Nicholas patted Andre on the back. "Thank you for finding this. Obviously, there's a message written with the blue flakes. But look, the red and green flakes combine to make a picture. I can't tell what it is yet, but maybe if we look at it long enough, we'll be able to see exactly what it is."

Andre agreed. "Read it to me, if you please."

Nicholas cleared his throat and prepared to speak. Andre knew he would use his *bishop's* voice that sounded warm and deep and authoritative. This always meant Saint Nicholas was about to say something very important. He cleared his throat again and began:

You are hereby, and very cordially invited, to a week-long visit in the North Pole, courtesy of Santa's Universal Family. Please bring appropriate attire and an appetite. We will be reuniting with other family members, so plan to share memories and old-time traditions as kin.

P. S. Don't forget the book!

"Well…well…well," Nicholas said and scratched his beard. "Now *that* is a message, indeed." He thought for a minute then glanced around the isolated acreage. "This gives me a better view and a wider perspective…and I see something, or rather someone, hiding there in the snow!"

"Santa and Nana Claus!" Andre gasped. "I need to tell the others!"

Nicholas chuckled, the trees jingled, and the reindeer snorted. "Come out, come out wherever you are!" Nicholas shouted. A resounding Ho-Ho-Ho! rang out as Santa recognized he'd been discovered.

"You found us faster than I thought you would, Nick!" Santa shouted back.

"This way…please come to the house and let's chat. We've much to catch up and discuss, apparently. Your message is clear but I still have questions…and my elves want to see their Nana."

Moments later, they were all seated in front of Saint Nicholas' massive fireplace, sipping wassail and munching on cookies. A dozen elves surrounded Nana Claus who sat next to a little elf with big brown eyes. She squeezed Nana's hand and shared a loving glance. "It's been too long since the brothers have seen each other." Though they worked well together during the holidays, they had been so busy that the family's rarely had a moment to spare for a visit," Nana said.

"Do you think it will work?" the little elf whispered to Nana Claus.

"I hope so. I'm doing my best to make sure everyone is there." With tears in her eyes and a soft-spoken voice, Nana replied, "Family time is the most important time."

The elves closed in and announced "We want to go too" in unison. They missed their cousins. Many of them had never shared a family reunion. "Please, let us go along too."

"Of course, you are all welcome. My other grandchildren will be so excited to see you!"

Nicholas cleared his throat—everyone knew what that meant. The room suddenly went silent. "Well, it seems, we have preparations to make if we are to make this journey with everyone in tow. There's much to be done, don't you agree Santa?"

Santa nodded. "Indeed, I do. Much to be done! You'll have to prepare your list a little early, Nick. Bring it with you when you come out and we can go over it together."

"But what about Peter? He has to review it too," Nicholas said, somewhat confused.

Santa winked. "Just bring the book. Trust me."

Nana Claus, Matilda, Santa, Mrs. Claus

Chapter Eleven

"**D**o you think they'll all make it?" Nana Claus asked Santa nervously as she straightened the tablecloth where business would be discussed over brunch and Matilda's delectables desserts. She'd been very busy lately without Katia around the kitchen to help. "I hope there will be enough food for everyone. You know how Black Peter loves my *Chocoladeletters*," Nana Claus added, glancing up at Santa.

"Yes, yes. That he does," Mrs. Claus agreed. But Santa didn't hear them, or so it seemed. So focused on a stack of papers, he was obviously distracted.

"Remind me to make certain that Matilda spells his name correctly. She tends to forget the *R* at the end of Peter." Nana shook her head and her curls bounced. "Goodness me!"

Nearly a week had passed since Thanksgiving and the messages had been delivered. Each of the cousins had indicated they would attend the reunion. Now, there was nothing to do but prepare for their arrival and wait.

As dusk arrived, Mavis (who had graciously stepped in for the absent Katia) put the finishing touches on a bouquet of poinsettias and holly, set impeccably in the front hall entry. She carefully dusted the bouquet with sugar to look like freshly fallen snow had just kissed the leaves. "There!" she announced. "That's the picture-perfect greeting for anyone who walks through the front door."

"Assuming they walk through the front door," Boris replied. He glanced at the fireplace. "You know how Peter likes to make an entrance."

"True!" Matilda's tiny voice called from the kitchen. "No one seems to use front doors anymore."

The elves nodded and sighed in unison. Predicting each of the cousins' arrival would be impossible. All they could do was prepare for any outcome. As a result, the house was decorated with poinsettias, holly, sprigs of mistletoe, and pine at every entryway. Nuts and dates had been positioned in key locations, mostly to keep hungry visitors from raiding the kitchen and spoiling Matilda's confections.

"I think it looks beautiful," Nana Claus announced.

"And it smells good too," Santa interjected.

Just then, a flurry of snow iced the windows and the sweet smell of cinnamon-sugar floated in the air. A tiny voice called out, "We're here!" as everyone turned to see the first guest walk through the front door and pause to glance at Mavis' poinsettia bouquet.

"Perfect!" the guest said as she entered and waved her hand at the decorations. "Everything is perfect."

"And *Lussekatter* will make it even more perfecter!" the tiny voice said as the door closed behind her.

As if in approval, the snow began to fall in giant flakes that sparkled with the kiss of the moonlight. The magic was about to commence!

Santa, Mrs. Claus, Nana Claus,
Black Peter, Saint Lucia

Chapter Twelve

Saint Lucia settled into the softest chair next to the fireplace. Snow wasn't something she had ever quite become accustomed to and the chill in the air gave her a little shiver.

"Here you are, Lucia," Mrs. Claus said, tucking a softly woven blanket across her lap. Matilda set a cup of steaming tea on the little table next to her. Lucia glanced at the fire burning inside brick and stone firebox, grateful for its warmth.

"Thank you, Mrs. Claus," Lucia said. "You know how to be the most gracious hostess to…" She stopped short and stared wide-eyed at the firebox. Bits of ash fluttered down, sprinkling the flames with soot. "What in the world?"

"I see it too," Matilda said, nearly dropping her tray.

The bits of ash grew larger in size and began to fall faster and faster, nearly snuffing out the flames. Within moments, heaps of ash covered the bottom of the firebox and doused the flames to nothing but curls of gray smoke. Just then, black boots landed smack-dab in the middle of the kindling, sending clouds of ash swirling onto the hearth.

"You better come…" *sneeze* "…and look at this, Santa," Nana Claus called out, covering her mouth and nose with her shawl. "Oh, dear!" she exclaimed and sneezed twice more.

Santa rushed into the room and clapped his hands with delight. "By Jove, it's Peter!" he exclaimed and bent his head toward the hearth in time to see knees, then hips, then the dark jacket he knew so well that belonged to Black Peter.

The cousins stood together, hands clasped in a hearty handshake as they clapped one another on the back. They were both covered in soot by now, Peter from head to toe and Santa's beard nearly as dark as the midnight sky.

"Come! Come in, Pete! It's so great to see you." Ash bounced off Peter's back as Santa gave him an extra clap. "You really do know how to make an entrance. Let's get you cleaned up a bit before brunch."

"And a mess on my floor too," Nana Claus winked behind the shawl that still covered her face.

"Oh, I'm so sorry, Nana. I forget what a mess I can be when I slide down chimneys. I don't know what Santa's secret is for doing that without all this soot!"

"Never you mind…we'll get this tidied up in a flash!" Mrs. Claus replied and motioned for help. Within seconds, Matilda and Boris appeared with brooms. Mavis held the dustpan and soon the floor was swept clean.

"I'm so glad you could make it, too," Saint Lucia said, taking a sip of her tea. "It's been so long, Peter."

He blew her a kiss from across the room and settled into a thick, leather chair. Matilda handed him a napkin heaped with sweetmeats and biscuits. "It was quite a trip," he said, "but I made it and I'm glad I did." He paused to look around the room. Two of his cousins were there but something was off. "Where is Saint Nick? He's supposed to be here too, isn't he?"

"Well, I suppose he ran into weather or something of the sort. You know how he can be…always late for a party." Santa said, glancing at Nana Claus who shrugged.

"I'm sure he'll be along soon," Lucia piped in. "Nicholas has *never* been on time to anything! He'd have been late for his own birthday if his mama hadn't been there first."

They all laughed but Santa wasn't amused. Nicholas had left at nearly the same time as Santa, and Nicholas' reindeer were the fastest team in the world. Something didn't feel right.

Santa stared out the window, watching for the glistening of the sleigh and tinkling of bells that always accompanied Saint Nicholas's travels but was met with only silence.

Yes, something was definitely off.

Mrs. Claus, Santa, Saint Nicholas,
Nana Claus, Black Peter, Saint Lucia

Chapter Thirteen

"**D**oes anyone see anything yet?" The little voice squeaked a bit as she asked the question on everyone's minds. Matilda jumped up and down, barely able to contain herself.

"Not yet," came a reply.

Four faces plastered against the oversized window peered out into the deepening sunset. Snow tickled the panes as the elves' breath fogged the glass with each excited outcry.

"He's sure to be arriving…any minute, now. We're just not seeing him. That's all it is." Matilda's voice suddenly sounded discouraged.

Nana Claus glanced at the elves lined up against the great window and shook her head. "They're right, you know. Nicholas should have been here by now."

Lucia sighed. "What do you supposed has happened."

"Oh, you know Nick! He's always distracted by something or other." Santa clicked his tongue against his teeth dismissively. "That Nicholas just can't stay focused…"

"Except when it comes to his book!" Nana Claus interjected. "Do you think something has happened to him… or to his list?"

Peter shifted in his seat and grunted. "I'll go find him," he stood then headed for the door…but stopped suddenly. "Better yet, I'll take the chimney. That'll get me up high enough to where I can better see Nicholas' sleigh…if he's still up there." Peter turned and tromped over to the fireplace. As he pulled a pouch from his jacket and readied to sprinkle ash to dampen the flames, the roof rattled and shook.

Crash! Bang! Followed by the *screech* of steel overhead that startled everyone, especially Peter who dropped his ash-pouch into the fire, dousing it with a loud *poof!*

"I think we have another visitor," Santa chuckled. "Mercy! That gave me a start. Nearly knocked my spectacles off entirely!" he said, re-centering his eyeglasses over his nose. He glanced at the roof then at Boris, who instantly jumped up.

"On it, boss," Boris said as he ran out of the room to help whoever had landed so clumsily on the roof. "I'll ask Gunnar to help, too."

Scrapes and scratches sounded above them, as if something very large and heavy was being dragged overhead. Soon, the sound of animals' paws and tromping footsteps moved along the length of the rooftop. Minutes later, the jingle of bells and a knock at the door let them know their long-awaited houseguest had finally arrived.

Santa threw open the door and exclaimed, "It's about time, Nicholas!" He grabbed his cousin and gave him a bear hug.

"Oh, yes, Nick." Nana Claus ran up and threw her arms around the jolly visitor. "We were so worried."

Lucia walked to where Saint Nicholas stood. "Please come join us Nick," she said and kissed his rosy cheek. "It's been so long!"

Nicholas chuckled and his "*Ho! Ho! Ho!*" rang out, sounding very much like the jingle of bells on his sleigh. He truly was a sight, covered in snow, his beard flecked with ice, and his nose rosy-pink. But the kind-hearted spirit that accompanied his arrival melted all thoughts of the cold night outside and warmed the cousins' souls. They were all together again, and that's what mattered.

"Welcome, Nick," Peter said, as he gathered his ash-pouch and placed it back into his jacket. "It just isn't the same without you."

Saint Nicholas chuckled again. "What a wonderful greeting to see all of you again. If it hadn't been for the problem with my book, I'd have been here sooner. But you know how lists can be."

Each of the cousins gave one another a knowing look. Mrs. Claus tugged on Nicholas' arm, urging him into the dining room alongside her.

"Come all. We have much to be thankful for," Nana announced, leading the way.

One by one, they entered the dining room and took their places around the table. The elves laid the last of the food in the center and joined them, sitting on chairs specially made for them. Nana nodded approval and smiled. "Indeed, we have so much to be thankful for. This is such a wonderful time to give thanks, just being together."

Everyone agreed: A wonderful time of Thanks-giving. "Let us pray and give thanks," Nana announced.

Mrs. Claus, Santa, Saint Nicholas,
Nana Claus, Black Peter, Saint Lucia

Chapter Fourteen

"Well, now, Nicholas," Santa leaned in and pushed his plate closer to the pudding bowl. "What seems to be the problem with your book?" He heaped another mound of chocolate walnut pudding onto his plate and focused on Nicholas, chomping on a spoonful of pudding as he listened.

"I couldn't believe it! Oh, it was awful!" Nicholas replied. "First, I had it in my hands and then the next thing I knew, it looked like this!" Nick held out a large book edged in gold fillagree and filled with thousands of pages lined with elaborately scrolled names, all alpha-betized. He opened the book midway through to reveal several torn pages. "Look! Will you just look at that?"

"What happened?" Santa exclaimed.

"It looks like someone took a bite out of your book, Nick," Peter interjected, leaning in to take a closer look. He lifted a monocle that was attached to his jacket pocket by a long, silver chain and placed it to one eye then peered closely at the book where the missing pages should be.

Nana Claus sniffed and wiped her cheek. "I'll get tea. Matilda, help me in the kitchen, will you dear?"

"I'll join you," Lucia said, jumping up from her chair by the fire.

"Me too," Mrs. Claus added, following them.

As they scurried off, Nana whispered, "This is going to be a very long night."

Nicholas began to pace. "As you can see, my *Book of Good Deeds* is ruined. I don't know what happened or where these missing pages could be. This is a disaster!"

Santa patted Nicholas' back, as he ambled by. "Well, it's a problem. You definitely need to consider better organization tactics, Nick."

Peter cleared his throat and caught Santa's eye, then shook his head. "I think what Santa is trying to say, Nick, is that we all feel your angst and are here to help you fix this problem. After all, we're family and I have the naughty list." He smiled a rather broad smile. "We will simply compare your book to my list and try to find the missing names."

"Yes! Yes! That! We will work together to solve this mystery," Santa chimed in.

Nicholas, still pacing, scratched the top of his head. "But I still don't know how this happened."

Just then, Gunnar stepped forward. "I believe those rough edges of paper resemble reindeer teeth prints. Perhaps the reindeer..."

"That's IT!" Nicholas exclaimed. "You are brilliant, Gunnar. I remember now! I was in the barn, readying my sleigh and team for the journey here. I must have set the book down and the reindeer, who seemed very interested in it, actually, must have…"

"Chewed out the missing pages!" Santa interjected.

There was a moment of silence as they all considered what to do next. One by one, they each began to walk, circling one another as they thought about the predicament they were in.

Suddenly, Peter stopped and looked at his cousins. "It'll be a treasure hunt! We'll look for clues and hopefully, recover some of the missing pages." He grasped Santa's shoulder and said softly, "Now, where do you keep the Claus Cam?"

Santa, Black Peter, Saint Nicholas

Chapter Fifteen

The *Claus-Cam* stayed locked up in a secret, specially sealed *Yuletide Vault*, tucked in the back of Santa's office. Rarely, was the *Claus-Cam* used, except for emergencies such as this one.

And indeed, they had an emergency, if ever an emergency existed.

"Follow me," Santa said and led his cousins to the office. He unlocked the door and moved through the room, stacked with red boxes tied in gold bows. A line of shelves held books just like Nicholas' *Good Deeds* book—the historical record of their work during the holidays. Gold and glass glittered from cabinets along the walls that sent shards of spectacular, glittering prisms in every direction. "In here," Santa said and pulled out another key, unlocking a hidden door that resembled a library bookcase.

As he opened the door, the hiss of fine mist that smelled like sugar cookies wafted out through its opening. "Impressive," Nicholas commented. "I must get one of these!" he said, lifting the velvet covering on a very unusual birdcage. The creature inside squawked and began to sing in music box notes.

"Don't touch that, Nick." Santa said, waving wildly. "You know better than to disturb a sleeping orchestrina passerine. They're very sensitive."

Nick nodded. "I forgot." He gently re-draped the velvet over the birdcage and the creature fell silent. "Sorry about that, Santa. I can get so distracted at times."

"Precisely your problem!" Peter said. "Now, let's try to figure out exactly what happened and just where those pages are."

The three cousins gathered around a small table made from teak that had been twinkle-coated to look like snow. No one cared that the table had arrived from Indonesia—a gift for *Sinterklas* from the people of Kampung Tugu during their traditional *Mandi-Mandi* celebration. Santa's face looked especially beautiful when painted white by the children, as was their custom during the holidays. The people were so proud that they gifted the teak-root table as a memento of their splendid time together. Santa treasured the table but only a little less than Nana Claus, who had insisted it be kept in the *Yuletide Vault* and used for very special occasions.

A sharp tap on the vault's doorframe startled them. *Ahem* then followed and Saint Lucia stepped lively to join them. "I see you're at work, dear family. And I'm glad that you are. This is quite precarious, as you know. But you cannot solve the riddle without me, of course," she said.

"Yes, yes, that's true," Santa agreed. "We cannot fully activate the *Claus-Cam* without her, of course."

All eyes darted to look at the oversized globe that suspended itself magically mid-air just a foot above the ground. Swirls of prism light and whisps of frosty currents churned inside the unusual orb.

"It's so beautiful!" Lucia exclaimed. "I nearly forgot how lovely is the *Claus-Cam*."

"Looks like an overgrown snow-globe to me!" Peter said, dropping his hands into his pockets. "Let's get on with it. We haven't much time…only a few weeks until the big day, and I still need to reference the Naughty List."

They all agreed and each cousin took their place around the *Claus-Cam*. One by one, they started to hum—a favorite holiday tune that resonated deep inside the enormous globe. Instantly, the prism colors shifted and the swirls danced in rhythm to their humming.

"Now sing," Santa said softly and each cousin began to sing the words to the family holiday carol.

It's a wonderful time of Thanks-Giving, Our family love keeps us living, Joy in our hearts, a rhythm of peace, Let's Pray and Bless this beautiful feast. Violin strings playing a melody sweet, Listen to our song, feel that soulful beat.

As if by magic, an image formed inside the *Claus-Cam*—slowly at first and then more clearly, it depicted a scene they instantly recognized.

"I think we have our answer," Santa announced, and peered deeper at the image brightening within the magical *Claus-Cam*.

Mrs. Claus, Santa, Saint Nicholas,
Nana Claus, Black Peter, Saint Lucia

Chapter Sixteen

"Isn't that your barn?" Lucia said, a bit flabbergasted Nicholas nodded. "Yes, unfortunately it is. I do remember setting down the *Good Deeds* book while inspecting the sleigh, but I don't remember what happened afterward."

Just then, a tiny elf ran through the image. Saint Lucia jumped. "What in the world was that?"

"Oh, Ho-Ho-Ho!" Nicholas chuckled. "That is one of the Ambassadors. He's a Good-Will Ambassador, if you will, because he only does good deeds and spreads great joy." They all gave him a look. "Around my property, that is. He is one of many very trusted ambassadors who help me." Nicholas glanced back at the *Claus-Cam* and scratched his head. "I guess he's doing good deeds in the barn today."

"That's it!" Pete exclaimed. "Why didn't I think of it before?" He took Nicholas by the shoulders. "We simply contact your ambassadors through the *Claus-Cam* and have them locate the missing pages in your *Good Deeds* book."

"Yes! I agree," Santa said. "That, in and of itself, constitutes a very good deed, if you ask me."

As if it understood them, the *Claus-Cam* began to glow. Santa moved to the controls and began to swipe across a screen. Images of the ambassadors began to blur then clear until it seemed as if they were standing in the same room. A light flashed inside the orb and one of the ambassadors stepped forward, then tapped a finger on a blinking light.

"Is that you, Santa?" the ambassador said, leaning in a little closer. His face looked huge in the *Claus-Cam* and his eyes appeared nearly as big as saucers. "Santa? Hello? Ambassador Baris here."

"Hello! Hello, Baris," Santa replied. "Yes, we're all here. Saint Nicholas as well."

Baris nodded and stepped back. He was quickly joined by four other elves. "I hear you loud and clear, Santa. What can we do for you?"

Nicholas stepped up to the edge of the *Claus-Cam* and spoke very loudly. "Hello? Can you hear me? Hello, Baris? Saint Nicholas here…" The elves all covered their ears, some wrinkling their noses and shutting their eyes. Santa tapped Nicholas on the shoulder and placed a finger to his lips. Thankfully, Nicholas got the message and lowered his voice. "I'm sorry about that, men. I forgot how sensitive the *Claus-Cam* can be. Is this better?"

The elf ambassadors nodded approval and smiled.

"Go ahead, Nick. Tell them what happened," Pete piped in.

Nicholas glanced at Pete then at Lucia, who nodded. "Go ahead, Nick."

"Well," Nicholas began. "You see…I lost a few of the pages from my *Good Deeds* book. I'm not sure what happened but they look like they were torn out."

"You mean, chewed out!" Pete said.

"*Ahem*…Yes, chewed out." Nick cleared his throat again. "I think I left the book there, on the haystack while I inspected my sleigh before the trip."

"The reindeer must have made nasty work out of the pages by now," Pete added.

Lucia placed her hand on Pete's arm. "Assuming the reindeer ate the pages," she added gently.

By now, the ambassadors had scattered, looking high and low for the missing pages…all except Baris who continued to man the *Claus-Cam*. Glancing over his shoulder, he could see the others snatching up pieces of white paper from the hay bales.

"It looks like we may have found the missing pages already. My team is excellent at hide-n-seek, and it appears they have found all of the pages that seemed to be hidden there." Baris pointed to the hay. "We'll have these gathered and sent to you directly. Do you prefer Turtle Dove Delivery or the French Hen Express?"

"Actually," Santa interrupted. "We're in a bit of a hurry. Could you just send it by *Claus-Cam* Photostat Copy?"

"I'll have Emir get on that right now. He's the most proficient with *Claus-Cam* Communications," Baris said.

Within moments, they could see Emir tap on the screen and seconds later, images of names scrolled in fancy manuscript appeared inside the *Claus-Cam*.

"There it is!" Nicholas said, clapping his hands. "Now we can get to work on our lists, aye Pete?" Nicholas winked at Black Peter, who nodded.

Lucia smiled. "The world is so distressed right now. We need to help turn it around. Thanks to Santa's *Claus-Cam*, we can do just that by bringing a spirit of love and unity for the holidays."

Just then, Nana Claus rushed into the room with Mrs. Claus close behind. "I think we may have a problem," Nana said. The object in her hand rustled as she trembled.

"What? What is it Nana?" Lucia said unable to hide the dread in her voice.

Nana glanced at Mrs. Claus then held out the object for all to see. They all peered at a photograph. "I believe we forgot someone."

"Actually, two *someone's*," Mrs. Claus replied, wringing her hands. A few gasps echoed inside the Yuletide Vault. "How did we ever forget them?" Mrs. Claus added.

Nicholas shook his head. "Quite the oversight!" Everyone looked at Nick who shrugged. "Well, I am forgetful, as you know."

The Season of change for Santa's Universal family was not yet complete. Nana Claus glanced down at the photo.

"Wherever did you find that, Nana?" Lucia said gently. "I'd nearly forgotten about that time."

"It was in my treasure chest—a real treasure indeed. Our family is more than just us. We must reach out to them…" She stopped mid-sentence.

Someone had entered the house.

Kente Claus and Papa Noel

Chapter Seventeen

The smell of warm tamales, fried rice, and beans drifted throughout the house, mingling with Lucia's warm cakes and cocoa. Bells sounded along with rattles that could only mean one thing.

"Yo, cuz! It's indeed a wonderful time of thanks-giving." The voice was deep, jolly, and inviting.

"Si! We bring gifts and food for all." A second voice called out, pitched higher and ever so cheery.

Everyone froze.

"Could it be?" Nana Claus cried out. "Are they really here?" She turned to look at the very faces captured on the photo in her hand.

"Is it really you?" Santa bellowed and rushed to greet them. "My dear, far-away cousins! Papa Noel and Kente Claus. I can't believe my eyes!"

Everyone rushed over to hug the two unexpected but very important cousins.

"Indeed, we have everyone together and can now celebrate a wonderful time of thanks-giving," Nana Claus said, wiping a tear from her cheek. "What a joyful, loving time of year!"

And in that instant, the *Claus-Cam* began to sparkle. Their work together had only just begun…

Additional books and music by Keith Stafford:

SANTA'S UNIVERSAL FAMILY TALES (a series)

"WHAT A WONDERFUL TIME
OF THANKSGIVING"
Available on all major streaming music platforms

Visit: Keith Stafford and Friends for more information.
www.KAS-Entertainment.com

About the Author

Keith A Stafford

Born in Philadelphia, PA, in the early '50s, Keith A. Stafford grew up immersed in a vibrant music scene, surrounded by industry professionals and artists. His musical journey began at age twelve, performing at local high school dances and talent shows. By age fifteen, Keith had recorded drums on his first record with *The Futures* and soon signed with Philadelphia International Records. As a professional entertainer, Keith toured iconic venues like the Apollo Theatre and the Lincoln Center, eventually taking his music around the globe. His career expanded into song-writing, producing, and arranging for the Life Group, alongside collaborations with major labels such as Warner Brothers and Atlantic Records. As a proud member of ASCAP,

Keith Stafford

Keith has continued to share his passion for music and the written word as a writer and publisher. Currently he is working with Belton Mouras Entertainment based in Sacramento, CA, as an international project and marketing manager, focusing on both film and music projects. Keith is thrilled to announce the release of his Holiday Single, *A Wonderful Time of Thanksgiving*, and the launch of his first children's holiday book series, *Santa's Universal Family Tales: A Family Reunion*. Keith's aim is to carve a unique niche in the entertainment world, sharing his contributions and experiences with others globally.